THE BOY
WITH WINGS

ATTACK OF THE RAMPAGING ROBOT

This book belongs to

....

I am a reader and I celebrated World Book Day 2023
with this gift from my local bookseller
and Macmillan Children's Books

Other books by Lenny Henry

The Boy With Wings

The Book of Legends

Lenny Henry

Illustrated by Keenon Ferrell

THE BOY WITH WINGS
ATTACK OF THE RAMPAGING ROBOT

MACMILLAN CHILDREN'S BOOKS

Published 2023 by Macmillan Children's Books
an imprint of Pan Macmillan
The Smithson, 6 Briset Street, London EC1M 5NR
EU representative: Macmillan Publishers Ireland Ltd, 1st Floor,
The Liffey Trust Centre, 117–126 Sheriff Street Upper
Dublin 1, D01 YC43
Associated companies throughout the world
www.panmacmillan.com

ISBN 978-1-0350-1592-4

1 3 5 7 9 8 6 4 2

A CIP catalogue record for this book is available from the British Library.

Printed and bound by CPI Group (UK) Ltd, Croydon CR0 4YY

With thanks to Holmen Paper and Gould Paper Sales for their support

WORLD BOOK DAY®

World Book Day's mission is to offer every child and young person the opportunity to read and love books by giving you the chance to have a book of your own.

To find out more, and for fun activities including the monthly World Book Day Book Club, video stories and book recommendations, visit **worldbookday.com**

World Book Day is a charity sponsored by National Book Tokens.

Prologue

Dark.

So dark, you couldn't see a hand in front of your face.

So dark, you don't even know if you've got a hand or a face to begin with.

As if floating in a starless space, suspended in a soupy jet-blackness.

That's how it felt.

And the funny thing was, the '*it*' in question had no idea **WHAT** *it* was. But then *it* thought to itself, even if *it* had no idea what *it* was, that must mean at some point in the recent past, *it* must have had **SOME** idea – which meant that *it* was able to **THINK**.

It thought for a moment, and asked itself a very important question:

'What am I doing here?'

It thought some more.

1

And then . . . *it* experienced a sensation. Several, in fact. The main one being that of absence. There was something MISSING. *Someone* . . . had removed a part of it. It was now feeling a burning sensation through its entire being. Anger.

And it thought to itself, with all the energy it could muster:

'WHO. HAS. DONE. THIS. TO. ME?'

It now knew that one thing was certain. Whoever *had* stolen a part of its being . . . they were going to pay.

CHAPTER ONE

Today was a special day.

Tunde Wilkinson was very dark-skinned with fluffy black hair and a slightly wonky, very beaky nose. His eyes shone with warmth and intelligence. He was also in possession of the most **magnificent wings** you've ever seen.

And, today, Tunde Wilkinson was turning thirteen!

He was trying to be happy because this was a day of celebration, but he was finding it a bit difficult. Most thirteenth-birthday celebrations happen at some kind of adventure park, the pictures, the aquarium or even in the wonky park equipped with the most dangerous slide in all the land. All parties of this kind involved cake and fizzy pop, sandwiches, chicken wings, popcorn, sweets, chocolate, biscuits, and even more cake. (Although his mother's idea of cake, if studied by the beardy bloke from *Bake Off*, would have raised an eyebrow. Tunde's mum saw cooking as an off-road adventure with no map, destination or steering wheel.)

Luckily for Tunde (and everyone else), Tunde's mum, Ruth had gone to the local supermarket and stocked up on '*shop-bought*' food (she muttered this as if she had just stepped in a Volkswagen-sized dog poo). So, there was no danger of squirrel and nettle pie with shortcrust pastry and a dusting of wasps washed down with stinky apple juice today. Thank goodness!

Tunde's birthday celebration was happening at The Facility, a big science complex on the outskirts of town where his mum and dad worked.

Professor Krauss, The Facility's never-ageing chief executive, had invited Tunde and his guests to celebrate in a lower laboratory area, because Tunde's house had recently been smooshed by an alien battleship and was now being rebuilt. It was kind of Professor Krauss, Tunde thought, but partying in The Facility because his family didn't have a house painfully reminded him that he had failed to defend their home.

Tunde tried to get himself in a party mood. His best friends were here! **He needed to cheer up, and fast.**

Nev Carter was Tunde's best buddy. They had fought side by side together, played football together – the only thing they couldn't do together was grow hair at the same rate. Nev's dreadlocks were almost down to his shoulders.

He grabbed Tunde by the shoulders. 'Oi, misery guts! We need to get the supermegalicious playlist on the sound system – this party's as dry as my back foot, cuz!'

Tunde cracked a smile. Nev had an unusual vocabulary and he liked to use it on every occasion.

'Nev, it's not really a dancing party. It's more an **"eat cake, drink fizzy pop, slurp jelly and then throw up"** kinda party!'

Nev pulled a face. 'Nobody better throw up on my new kicks, bruv, or it'll be like battle stations, innit?'

Jiah, Tunde's bespectacled, maths-loving nerd-in-arms, approached now. But she wasn't only a mathlete. She also read comics to try to work out if you could actually build a flying suit of armour or invent shoes that allowed you to jump several miles at a time.

Jiah took Tunde to one side. 'Tunde,' she whispered. 'There's a load of rooks outside trying to form themselves into a feathered sign that says **HAPPY BIRTHDAY**. You should probably tell them to stand down before someone notices.'

'Nah.' Tunde loved his shared connection with all kinds of birds. 'Let 'em do it. I like it when they pass on messages like that.'

'But there's *thousands* of them,' Jiah insisted. 'The message is about a mile high. You'd be able to see it from space.'

Tunde closed his eyes and sent a message to the birds with his mind. 'They've gone now. The chief rook who organized it said to tell you you're a snitch,' he teased her.

'There's no need for that kind of language. At least I don't eat worms!' Jiah replied.

'You don't know what you're missing then!' Tunde laughed. 'They're all chewy and gooey and . . .'

Jiah made an 'I'm about to do a technicolour yawn in a minute if you don't shut your gob' face and turned her back on him.

Kylie was listening to the whole thing just

behind them. She was also coming over to tell Tunde to buck up and get with the party vibes.

'You know,' she said, 'anyone'd think you hated birthdays.'

Tunde thought for a second. 'I don't hate birthdays. It's just that this time last year everything kicked off and didn't stop kicking off until we were all in space fighting angry cat aliens.'

'Gosh, yes! That was fun,' said Kylie. 'I know we nearly got blasted to smithereens, but that was an adventure. I miss us playing the game to learn more about **S.H.I.P.P.E.** (the Sentient Hyper-Intelligent Pan-Planetary Entity – aka the spaceship). Are we going to start doing that again soon?'

'I dunno, Kylie,' Tunde replied. 'We probably shouldn't be wishing for adventures and space travel and stuff. Those cat things attacked our house and destroyed the den. Mum was nearly—'

'But she wasn't!' Dembe, the newest member of the gang, interrupted. Tunde's parents had recently offered to act as her new step-parents. 'You saw off the alien attackers. We're safe because we've all got each other's backs.'

'We all watch out for each other,' Kylie agreed.

Tunde wasn't sure. 'What if you guys get hurt because of me, though? I don't think I'd be able to stand it if I got you into more trouble.'

Dembe ran her hands through Tunde's hair. 'Only thing that's gonna get you in trouble is your manky hair – you need to get some dreads like Nev!'

Kylie laughed. Nev overheard Dembe and flicked his head so his locks wriggled like snakes.

Tunde smiled. His friends were all right, and he was happy they were there.

Professor Krauss chinked on his glass with a teaspoon – a signal to all concerned that he was about to make a speech to the small group of guests.

'Tunde, I'm so pleased to be here today, celebrating your birthday with your parents, who are amongst my best scientists. Ruth, you're one of my top bio-engineers here, and Ron, you're of course a leader in your field.'

Ron grinned. 'I work with vegetables – I'm always in a field, me.' Tunde groaned at his dad's joke.

Professor Krauss continued: 'Tunde, you and your friends: Nev, Jiah, Kylie and Dembe, went all the way into space, took on an attacking alien force, and won!' Tunde saw his friends beaming with pride.

Nev did a little dance and started chanting like he was Beyoncé.

'Who saved the world? US! Who saved the world? US!'

Professor Krauss raised a glass of fizzy water. 'You actually DID save the world! And no one in Ruthvale has the foggiest idea what you did. You and your friends are heroes, Tunde!'

THERE WAS A MASSIVE CHEER.

The professor wrapped up: 'Now, enjoy yourselves – this is a party! Eat, drink, celebrate! I believe Nev has something called a "dope-a-licious playlist" that he wants us to shake our hips to. Mine are plastic, so I might not join you.'

Everyone laughed at that. Krauss continued: 'But don't go anywhere you shouldn't. I can't vouch for your safety.'

Everyone *half* laughed at that, knowing it was probably true. (The Facility housed some weird, wonderful and SUPER-dangerous stuff; all manner of laboratory-raised animals, minerals and vegetables . . . WEIRDSVILLE.)

Ron came over and ruffled his son's hair. 'I'm so proud of you, son. Have I told you that yet today? You're like one o' them super-dudes, but from just outside Birmingham!'

Tunde looked at the floor 'It wasn't just me. *Everybody* helped.' It was true; his friends' quick learning of the alien technology that The Facility's team had transported to Earth had made them a group of 'intergalactic-tastic alien bum-kickers', as Nev had named them all.

Tunde shuffled his feet and continued. 'Dad, I can do more. To help, I mean. I want to! When those monsters attacked the house and hurt Mum's arm, I should have been able to protect you.'

'*You* saved my life,' Mum said. 'And look, this arm *was* hurt badly, but Professor Krauss helped me to rebuild and redesign it. I can do things with this arm now that I could never do before.' Mum pulled up her sleeve to reveal a newly rebuilt, **HIGH-TECH ROBO-ARM**.

Tunde gingerly touched his mum's arm, marvelling at its lifelike quality. 'That's amazing. What else are you working on here? Can I have a look?'

Ron flashed Ruth a worried glance, and she brushed Tunde off with: 'Everything's boring as usual here. Booooring! Nothing you need to worry about, darling. Nothing to see here at all.'

Ron nodded his agreement. 'Yep. Nothing to see here at all. Absolutely nothing of interest. You run along now and do some kerplunking to this loud music!'

Ruth looked confused. 'It's a kind of dance,' Ron explained. 'I saw it on television. Young people do it in Los Angeles. Kerplunking.'

Tunde looked at them and laughed. 'He's right, Mum.'

Dembe had been listening the whole time and gave Tunde a nudge as they both headed over to the overfull buffet table and snaffled a paper plate full of chicken wings, little vegetarian pies and an apple.

'It's *krumping,* you nana,' she said, and laughed.

'I know,' Tunde said. 'But I didn't have the heart to tell him.'

'Why don't they want you looking around?'

'I dunno. Maybe they're scared I'm gonna find out that my birth parents are alien bird creatures?'

'But you already know that!' Dembe replied.

'I know,' Tunde agreed. 'What else is there to find out! I wish they wouldn't hide things from me.'

'They're just trying to protect you, Tunde,' she said. 'Now let's enjoy your party. Nev's playlist is **BANGING**.'

And it was. But Tunde was too confused to kerplunk or krump. His mind whirled with questions. Since when did Mum and Dad not want to talk about their new projects? Why were they being so mysterious? His friends were on the dance floor throwing nerdy shapes to Nev's mixtape, but Tunde kept thinking aloud to Dembe.

'What's the point of having powers if I can't use them? Right now I'm just a kid with wings, doing normal stuff like going to school and hanging out and playing computer games, just waiting for the next monster to come and threaten us all. Well, the next time it happens I want to be ready. Why won't they let me *help people?*' Tunde's voice was getting louder.

Dembe looked up and saw hundreds of rooks looking down through the skylight, tweaking their heads from left to right, and flapping furiously. She nudged Tunde. 'Your bird mates are getting all tetchy. It's your birthday, relax!'

'I can't just relax! I've been listening to police radio on **S.H.I.P.P.E.** at night, scanning to see if anybody needs help and then,' he confessed, 'I've been going off and helping them.'

Jiah, who had given up trying the new and ridiculously complicated dance that Nev had seen online, overheard and joined the conversation.

'Tunde, you know you might draw attention to yourself if you're out fighting crime?'

As the one who was most enthusiastic about sciencey-type stuff, Jiah had spent more time than everyone else learning as much as possible about **S.H.I.P.P.E.** and what it could do. But not even she knew that Tunde had been using **S.H.I.P.P.E.** for this purpose.

'She's not just a radio, you know? **S.H.I.P.P.E.** is a very complicated craft, and you shouldn't be using her to listen to criminals breaking into warehouses or whatever it is you've been doing.'

Tunde grinned at her and blurted out, 'I got a cat down from a tree.'

'It was at least two hundred feet up in the air,' he explained. 'I don't know how it got up there. Maybe a hot air balloon? It could have been a bungee jump gone wrong!'

Now Kylie and Nev joined them to listen to their friend.

Kylie was a bit shocked. 'What's going on,

Tunde? Sounds like you want people to know there's a boy with wings out here.'

'I'm doing good things!' Tunde insisted. 'This creep stole a pensioner lady's purse, and some magpies and I got it back. He won't be doing that again. His bum got pecked to kingdom come!'

Tunde was laughing now.

Kylie, Nev, Jiah and Dembe were looking more and more concerned. Dembe piped up, 'Were you just . . . y'know . . . flyin' around in broad daylight doing this stuff?'

Tunde was all excited. 'I can't help it. The other day, I got several hundred ducks to tow a bloke from the middle of the reservoir after he'd capsized his boat. The guy wanted to pay me – and one of the ducks said he could put it on his bill!'

Everyone cracked up at this – everyone except for his mum and dad, who had also been listening in on Tunde's adventures. Ruth's face was a picture of barely concealed anger.

'You've been flying around at all hours of the day and night . . . having adventures? Without even bothering to cover up your face?'

'I wear a mask!' said Tunde, defending himself.

His mum wasn't having it. 'Don't people get frightened when this – this – this – *mask-wearing maniac with wings* comes zooming towards them?'

'This isn't what we agreed, Tunde,' Dad said. He sounded serious.

Tunde started shifting from foot to foot nervously.

Mum's eyes glistened with tears. 'Tunde, we adopted you. You're our son and we love you. But your powers are a secret and have to stay that way. We can't have you making a spectacle of yourself. It's too **dangerous** for you AND it's dangerous for all of us who know you.'

Tunde looked at her. 'What do you mean?'

'Every time something happens around here, whether it involves you or The Facility, the folk that live in this area have to be made to forget it,' Dad explained. 'It's powerful technology – we don't want to scramble too many brains. We could end up with a town full of zombie Ruthvalians who can't remember where they live or how to use a knife and fork.'

Tunde looked at his feet. He hadn't even considered how his superhero activities could affect the townsfolk. Mum cupped his face in her hands and made sure to look him in the eye. 'Promise me you won't do this again?'

'I promise, Mum,' Tunde agreed.

Mum and Dad left to let him go back to his friends. Nev immediately got him in a bear hug. 'Bro, you look like someone's slapped you with one of them giant rubber hands, like **blapblapblapblapblap!**'

Dembe laughed. 'We're clearly not keeping you busy enough at football practice if you're so vexed that your mum and dad won't let you go out to fight crime.'

Kylie's face had softened and become all glowy and caring. She took his arm. 'Tunde, d'you want to talk about it? Shall we form a chat circle? We can use my pencil for a talking stick.' Kylie's mother was a therapist who used cushions for her clients to weep or scream into, and talking sticks for either one of them to hold (which meant the other person had to keep their gob shut).

'I wonder if they've got any chamomile tea here?' she continued.

It was all too much for Tunde.

'I don't WANT any chamomile tea! I just want to help!' Tunde exploded. 'Why can't I do that? The heroes in the comics go out at night and help people *all the time*. Why can't I?'

'Bro, it's one thing to save the world when you *have* to,' Nev counselled gravely, 'but maybe you shouldn't go *looking* for trouble. You get me?'

Jiah nodded. 'The probability of you being vaporized by some alien dinosaur creature increases every day *just because you exist*!'

'And health-wise,' Kylie mused, 'it's probably not good to run around at night in your underwear with a target on your back.'

'Exactly. You're not indestructible, you know.' Dembe sighed. 'You should go round to everybody and just say sorry for bein' a complete and utter doofus.'

Tunde gave up. 'All right, all right! I'm going back to the party.'

Tunde set about opening his presents from everyone. He began with Jiah's gift; she had sent away for the matching jumper to a pair of Mathsox she had bought him the year before. Tunde now was the proud possessor of a purple jumper with complex mathematical problems stitched in silver thread over its entire surface.

'It's the perfect revision tool,' Jiah insisted.

Dembe laughed. 'Who revises with a jumper? It's the geekiest thing ever! And I live at Tunde's house where geeks go for their holidays.'

Kylie laughed. 'Yeah, but only for the *geek-end*.' Everybody groaned.

All the birds watching from above seemed to relax, as if it were that moment of tranquillity just before a huge and devastating storm.

Which was exactly what was about to happen.

CHAPTER TWO

Tunde's family lived two stops on the bus route out of Ruthvale in the South Midlands.

Ruthvale was a large town; not as big as the local market town up the road with its canals and a zoo, and nowhere near as small as some of the other neighbourhoods in the Midlands, some of which couldn't even muster a halfway decent bowls team.

Ruthvale had its own kind of cool.

There was a bookshop called Once Upon A Wow, a pet shop called Grrrr, and a specialist Jamaican hairdresser's called Plaits All Folks!

(Ruthvale also boasted one of the most dangerous adventure playgrounds ever created. The ropes on the swings regularly detached mid-swing, causing small children to fly into the nearest soft hedge, and the slide had completely rusted so that anyone daring to clamber up there might come down completely encased in brown dust.)

The local school, St Pritchett's, resembled a mini cathedral and, over the years, had acquired many prefab extensions to accommodate the hundreds of extra pupils that continued to flow in from all points of the compass.

Tunde and his friends had **SURVIVED** life at St Pritchett's by sticking together as much as they could and having each other's backs.

That day, Mr Beeston (of the baggy suit and exploding haircut) was making the class use something called the *Encyclopaedia Britannica*. This was a brilliant old series of enormous textbooks that contained all the information you need about anything. Mr Beeston enthused about how, before the internet, these books were what human beings referred to when they wanted to know something.

Jiah loved the idea of a book with unending information. 'Just imagine! A set of books that contain megatonnes of information so that anyone can just pick them up at the library and be able to know *anything*.'

Tunde thought this was hilarious. 'I like the idea of a load of books with all this information in them, Jiah, but there's this thing called the internet? It's free!'

Dembe and Nev looked at each other, and muttered, 'Can't believe we're in the nerd gang.'

Kylie stared at them both. 'It wouldn't kill you to open a book occasionally, you know.'

Nev scoffed. 'Bro, man don't need books, man's got magic feet.'

Dembe nodded. 'When I'm a Billionaire Superstar Fashionista I'll remind you about when you told me how vital encyclopaedias were going to be to my life.'

Jiah couldn't believe what she was hearing. 'But books are brilliant. **Books are fun.** They're so full of . . . information! I wish I owned a library! If I did, I'd make you come every day and take out books and books and books! Then you'd see!'

Nev looked at Dembe, and Tunde laughed. They wrestled the enormous books back to their workspaces and cracked them open.

That day there was a new boy in class: Artie Fisher. He was the same age as Tunde, but lighter-skinned with a pudgier nose. He had two stringy braids on either side of his face and two slightly thicker ones hanging down the back of his head.

Tunde glanced across the room and caught Artie's eye. Artie grinned back at him with all his teeth.

Nev laughed. 'Bro, that new kid needs to chill. He's way too keen.'

Kylie elbowed him, 'Don't be mean! I'm going to find him at lunchtime and make sure he's OK.'

And then they heard Quinn Patterson, St Pritchett's biggest bully, saying 'NOW!'

Pauly Gore was the lead muscle in Quinn Patterson's gang. Although Sanjay Khan was Quinn's number two and Billy Willis was also tough and quick, Pauly was the one you sent in like a humanoid wrecking ball to knock everything down.

Quinn had spotted Tunde's feet sticking out to the side of his desk and sent Pauly down the aisle holding three encyclopaedias over his head, clearly aiming at Tunde's toes. Tunde looked up in time to yell, 'Gore, what are you d—'

When, suddenly, Artie Fisher threw himself across the room, caught the books and flung them back at Pauly, who took the hit directly in the chest and ker-boinged into a nearby bookcase! **KER-BOOIIIIING!**

The whole classroom erupted into laughter, apart from Quinn Patterson and his disbelieving cronies. Mr Beeston hoicked Pauly to his feet and ordered Artie to re-stock the bookshelf: **'NOW!'**

Nev caught Dembe's eye and nodded. Then they, Jiah and Kylie all rushed across to help Artie.

Tunde was in shock. He watched his friends chatting to Artie as they helped him stack shelves with speed and efficiency. *Who is this kid?* he thought to himself.

Something about the colossal spurt of speed that propelled Artie across the room somehow didn't seem right.

The bell rang and Tunde filed outside behind his friends.

Quinn Patterson was waiting in the corridor for him.

'Hey Beak-a-zoid! There's no need for yer man to jump in and catch them books. You could have just batted them away with your ginormous hooter.'

Billy doubled over with braying laughter. 'Yeah, if you'd just *breathed out,* you'd have blown the books *and* Pauly to the moon.'

Sanjay bellowed. '*Yeah, smothered in bogeys.*'

Dembe pulled a face. 'You lot should be on the stage – one leaves in two minutes. Why don't you all just leave us alone?'

Billy Willis glared at her. 'Why don't you shut your face?'

Dembe flexed. 'Why don't you try and make me?'

Kylie wheeled in between them, clasped her hands together and said, 'I think we should all take a *deeeeeeeeep breath:* let's breathe IN for four, three, two, one, and OUT for four, three, two, one . . .'

Patterson poked Tunde in the chest. 'This is the most useless collection of geeks anybody's ever had. Are they supposed to have your back?'

Tunde bristled, knowing that, if he wanted to, he could flex his wings right now and whap Patterson upside the head multiple times. He took a deep breath and opened his mouth to say something back when, out of nowhere, Artie Fisher popped up between him and Patterson . . . grinning. 'Why d'you keep poking him in the chest? Do you think he's a loaf of bread? Are you checking to see if he's done?'

Patterson did **NOT** look pleased. Artie continued: 'You know, if you don't want to be bezzy friends, you should try country dancing.' He grabbed Patterson's hand tightly and proceeded to spin him around, then hopped and skipped towards Pauly Gore and somehow spun him around like a top too. He ran circles around all of Quinn's gang, who stormed off in four different directions, then stormed back and tried to storm off in the same direction.

The rest of the kids in the corridor started laughing at Pauly, Sanjay, Billy and Quinn Patterson walking dizzily. 'Country dancing!' Artie exclaimed. 'It's good! You might not be able to walk straight for an hour, but at least you've had your daily exercise.'

Nev patted Artie on the shoulder. 'Bruv, that was quality.'

Kylie shook her head but couldn't help smiling. 'I don't usually believe in violence, but what you just did was **mega-quality**.'

'Agreed. Respect, new kid.' Dembe held out her fist for a bump.

Artie bumped her back and then headed for Tunde, who was standing there, shaking with fury.

'What are you angry about?' Artie asked, confused. 'He was bullying you and I helped.'

Kylie, Dembe, Nev and Jiah all nodded their heads in agreement.

Tunde looked at them, then at Artie. 'I don't

need you to rescue me, thanks very much. I can look after myself. If everyone would just leave me alone, I could . . .' Tunde groaned in frustration and stomped off. Artie's face was full of disbelief. Kylie wheeled herself across to him. 'You'll get used to him. He's one of my best friends, but he's a **gold medal** sulker when he wants to be.'

'Sulking is a sign from inside that there is future pain to be dealt with,' Artie replied, wisely.

'That's amazing,' Kylie said. 'That's exactly what it says in one of my mum's books.'

Nev came up, admiring Artie's braids. 'I'm liking your locks, bruv.'

'You need to get down to Plaits All Folks.' Artie smiled. 'They do plaits, extensions, braids – the works. Momma Lakeesha is skiz-elled to the mi-zax.'

Dembe, meanwhile, had gone back to flicking through inspirational design pictures on her phone. Artie clocked them immediately: 'Banksy is dread, Basquiat is well cool, and Picasso was a G.' Dembe flushed. Artie nodded and continued: 'Can you imagine how Picasso might have designed streetwear?'

And as Tunde's posse chittered, chattered and were flattered by Artie Fisher – this NEW kid – Tunde sat on a tree stump in the playground and bit his lip hard, trying to control his feelings. For goodness' sake! He was Earth's Guardian. He had superpowers. *He could fly*!

Who did Artie Fisher think he was, trying to protect Tunde Wilkinson?

CHAPTER THREE

The next day, Tunde woke up early. A magpie had taken to tapping on his window at 6.45 a.m. every morning. Tunde had been annoyed at first, but had soon realized that the old saying, 'The early bird catches the worm', actually made a lot of sense. When you got up early, you could get ahead of the day: finish your homework from the night before, play a sneaky game on your computer or snaffle the last secret bowl of Chunky Explody Cocoa Puffs before anyone else was up.

Sometimes, he would sneak up to his mum's lab and look through the keyhole. Her workshop was an Aladdin's cave containing multiple computers, half-finished inventions and signed pictures of unusual chefs from around the world.

Looking through the keyhole was as close as he could get to Mum's lab now. She used to allow him to watch her work on the weekends, but more recently she had started turning him away and refusing to let him see what she was doing. He knew it was something to do with The Facility and the recent attack by creatures from another dimension. And he also knew that whatever she was doing often blew out all the lights in the neighbourhood. What he didn't know was why *he* wasn't allowed to get involved. He was **The Boy with Wings**. Surely that had to count for *something*?

He was determined to find out what his mum was up to, and so Tunde began to slyly try to find out more from Dad. The best time to do this was at the weekend in their super-landscaped garden, which was as neatly trimmed as a Belgian detective's moustache. Lately Ron had been growing mutant hydrangeas, each one the height of a Russian boxer, and prize-winning marrows, which had insides that tasted vaguely of steak (the owner of the local supermarket asked Ron to help them create a line of non-meat dishes entitled 'The Contrarian Vegetarian').

Whenever Tunde cornered his dad in the garden, however, Ron would simply *pepper* him with jokes.

'Tunde! What do you call a deer with no eyes? *No-eye deer!* Get it? No i-dea! . . .

Tunde! I'm worried about that calendar upstairs. *Its days are numbered.*

Come on, son! These are gold! You could go on the Royal Variety with them. I've got another one.

What did one hat say to the other? *"Stay here, I'm going on a-*head.*".* . . .

Why didn't the skeleton climb the mountain? *It didn't have the guts* . . .

Why did the scarecrow win an award? *Because it was out-standing in its field.*'

And then Dad would run around in a circle with arms aloft as if he'd just scored the winning goal at the World Cup final.

Tunde would just stand there with a **silly grin** on his face. He knew his dad spent hours on the internet looking for jokes that Tunde might not have heard. (Often, Tunde *had* heard them, but he would laugh anyway because he loved to see Dad enjoying himself.)

At breakfast that morning, while Dembe glared at Tunde for finishing the last of the Chunky Explody Cocoa Puffs, Mum reminded him that he should keep an eye on his emotions during the big football match later. She was right to be wary; Dogwall Comprehensive had trounced St Pritchett's six-nil last year. Mr Grierson, the sports teacher, had been training them so hard for today's game all the defenders had burst into tears and texted their parents in protest. Tunde, however, couldn't wait to get on the pitch.

Mum looked at him beadily. 'You know what happens if you don't stay calm during the match, don't you? You'll suddenly sprout wings in the middle of a half-volley.'

'Let's see any of the Lionesses do that!' Dad laughed.

'I bet they could! The Lionesses rule!' Dembe replied, and then started singing a song about 'Three Lionesses on the Shirt'.

Tunde loved football too. He had played in lots of matches since the day he'd discovered he had wings. Thankfully, everyone who'd seen him hovering, FIFTEEN FEET IN THE AIR, had had their memory erased by The Facility.

'Nev says . . .' And then Tunde did a near-perfect impression of his friend. "'Bruv. We can beat Dogwall without you having to sprout dirty great wings, cuz!" So don't worry,' Tunde reassured his parents. And then he hugged them both, grabbed his rucksack, and he and Dembe left for school.

Sometimes Tunde didn't join Dembe on the bus and ran to school instead. He didn't jog so fast that his wings popped out of his jacket and blasted him off and up into the sky at great speed, he jogged just quickly enough to **bring joy to his heart**. As he moved, he looked and saw sparrows flying overhead, almost as if they were watching over him. Six crows joined him and flew alongside. A plethora of thrushes flew towards, around and under him.

He kept jogging whilst laughing at the same time. 'You guys are all over me today. Give me some room.' But the sparrows, crows and thrushes continued to fly almost in formation around **the boy with wings**, who had no idea why they were being so attentive today.

When he reached the gates, the birds exploded in a feathered firework of activity. They swirled

around the school and then dispersed. Tunde shook his head, and muttered, 'Like they've never seen this place before.'

He headed straight into pre-game training, where Mr Grierson set out how they were going to play. No one ever questioned Mr Grierson, because he was huge and muscular (like a balloon full of walnuts); but mainly because he was a good coach, and today he was giving them pointers about how to completely smash Dogwall Comprehensive.

Nev, Dembe and Tunde all played up front and were a good team: Nev was able to score with both of his feet, and he kept super-chill if things weren't going St Pritchett's way; Dembe had no fear of taking penalties, and never backed down from a crunching tackle; and Tunde seemed to know instinctively where to be to receive a pass – plus, he never stopped moving.

Unfortunately, Quinn Patterson was also one of their **BEST STRIKERS** and, unsurprisingly, very selfish. He held on to the ball as if his feet were superglued to the thing. He rarely passed and always went for the goal himself. (And whenever Patterson *did* score, his celebration was a complex mime about digging to the centre of the Earth and right through to Australia. It took a while.)

Usually they all rotated through the upfront positions, and Nev, Dembe and Tunde had worked out (between themselves) how to navigate their way around selfish Quinn. Now, though, Mr Grierson told the rest of the team, 'Everybody, we have a *new* striker!'

Artie walked onto the pitch, smiled his winning smile and, having received a volley from Dembe, did the most amazing overhead kick anyone had ever seen outside of YouTube.

'New rule: get the ball to the new kid!' Mr Grierson demanded, before sending them to run laps.

'That was amazing, bruh,' Nev said as they ran alongside each other. Dembe caught up to the two of them, easily matching Artie's speed. They all chattered away, thick as newly minted thieves . . . and Tunde jogged slowly, sulkily, behind them.

When the match finally began, it was a **BIGGER CROWD** than usual because the school's electricity had blacked out and refused to come back on. All the rooms were dark, and the Wi-Fi had gone AWOL. So the Headteacher went round all the classes and said, 'Shall we just all go and watch the match?' The resulting cheer could have been heard on the moon.

Soon, both teams were warming up on the pitch. Dogwall Comprehensive players sported their away kit, which was green with black horizontal stripes.

'Like playing a load of humbugs with arms and legs,' Dembe said, nodding in their direction.

Nev pointed towards a very tall centre forward with a long ponytail of dreadlocks. 'He's got some height on him. Look at them legs. Man's like a giraffe in shorts.'

Dembe searched out her opposite number on the team, a wiry girl with a fringe and freckles doing one-handed press-ups on the centre spot. She'd reached fifty before the ref sounded the whistle for them to start the game. Nev raised an eyebrow at Dembe: 'Good luck with her.'

Tunde kept his mouth shut. He was focused on the game and nothing else.

The referee, a blonde lady with wire-rimmed

glasses and beady eyes, ran a fair game, which was excellent for St Pritchett's. From the minute proceedings began, One-Handed Press-Up Girl had successfully stopped Dembe's runs repeatedly by tackling like a bulldozer with attitude.

'What're you gonna do about her?' Nev asked.

'She's gonna get a yellow card and then a red card, ain't she?' Dembe replied.

'Let's hope so, otherwise you're gonna be stretchered off, innit?' Nev said.

Meanwhile Patterson kept up a running commentary about Tunde's efforts. 'Oh, and here's Streaky Beaky. He's fast, but a bit like Cinderella – he never gets to the ball.'

Tunde was getting more and more frustrated. He hijacked the ball from a too-casual midfielder and attempted a run at goal. Then the Giraffe Kid got the ball away from him! Patterson couldn't contain his laughter.

Suddenly Artie Fisher was there. Artfully robbing the ball back from the lanky kid and passing to Tunde with a flourish. Tunde smacked the ball to Nev. Nev lobbed it back to Tunde. Patterson was in the goal area, surrounded by defenders, forwards, the goalkeeper, and one or two pigeons.

Everyone was wedged to the right-hand side. Tunde saw his chance. He flipped the ball into the air . . . and with all the time in the world, almost levitating, whacked the ball into the left side of the net! It was a **Goooooooaaalllll!!!!**

The ref blew the whistle for half-time.

Tunde, beaming, ran back to the halfway line, huffing and puffing a little. As he waited for the rest of the team to join him and celebrate, Artie Fisher was suddenly in his face. 'Just checking

you're all right.' He then handed Tunde what looked like a six-litre container of water. 'Make sure you rehydrate. You look a bit hot out there.'

Patterson came off the pitch next. 'Ahhhhh, look at you two! You're sure you don't want a teensy-weensy nap, Beakzilla? It's only half-time and your buddy's already advising yer to have a week's holiday.'

Tunde brusquely refused the water bottle and yelled at Artie, 'Leave me alone!'

Shortly after the second half kicked off, the lanky kid (his name was Ferdinand, for those who really want to know) had had enough of being one-nil down. In long, loping strides, his feet ate up the St Pritchett's half of the pitch. It didn't matter that Nev was talented, it didn't matter that Dembe was shifty and wily on the ball, it didn't matter that Tunde never stopped running, because, in this vital moment, Ferdinand played a blinder and whomped the ball into the **back of the net**, equalizing for Dogwall, who then went on to hold the St Pritchett's team at one-all for the rest of the game.

No matter what they did, Tunde, Nev, Dembe and even Quinn Patterson were frustrated by

Dogwall's persistence. **They wouldn't give up.**

Soon it was the dying minutes of the game. Patterson was showing off, the ball at his feet, zigging and zagging and commentating at the same time. 'Patterson's got the ball now, he's playing brilliantly, there's no one near him . . .'

But there was, actually. A squat defender ran at him and almost separated Quinn's knees from the rest of his body. Ouch-a-roonie! (Even though later Quinn boasted that 'it didn't really hurt. I've had harder kicks from my baby brother.')

It was a St Pritchett's free kick.

Nev set up for the kick. Dembe, Artie and Tunde were in place.

Whichever one of them got the ball, the plan was to snake round the nearest defender and try to get the ball to whoever looked on shot. Dembe got the ball and whipped it round to Tunde, but it was too high, it'd have to be a volley. Tunde hurled himself into the air, and everything in him wanted to continue soaring upwards, release his wings and fly six times around the school in a victory salute. Tunde was just about to head the ball when out of nowhere Artie flew in, backward bicycle-kicking the ball right into the top left-hand corner of the net!

Mr Grierson was up and yelling to the rest of the school.

'It's flippin' TWO-ONE! TWO-ONE TO ST PRITCHETT'S! IT'S TWO-ONE!!!'

Nev, Dembe and the rest of the team hugged Artie Fisher and began throwing him up in the air, chanting, 'Ar-tie, Ar-tie Fisher, la la la la laaaaa, la la laaaaaa!'

Quinn Patterson stood fifty feet away from all this commotion, pretending to yawn.

TUNDE COULDN'T BELIEVE WHAT HAD HAPPENED!

That was *his* goal.

He stomped off back towards the school, ignoring the St Pritchett's crowd who were all in the process of leaping, yelping, screaming, turning cartwheels and roly-polies.

Artie chased after Tunde whilst peeling a large orange. 'Wait! You really should top up with some vitamin C! Have some of my orange . . .'

'Why can't you just leave me alone?!' Tunde glared at him. 'That should have been MY goal!'

Dembe and Nev caught up with them just in

time to see Tunde yelling at Artie. Jiah and Kylie, who had been watching the match from the sideline, had also just come over to see what was going on. Tunde pointed a finger at Artie accusingly.

'He stole my goal!'

'You both scored, what's the problem?' Kylie asked.

'Right, bruv, he was only trying to help,' Nev agreed. 'And we WON!'

'And you were showing off anyway.' Dembe nudged Tunde, trying to tease a laugh out of him.

'Yes, you hovered in the air for at least five seconds longer than you should have.' Jiah looked around, then whispered. 'People might suspect something.'

Tunde looked at his friends and shook his head, 'You're supposed to be on my side. You're the only ones who know who I am! Playing football like this is like having one hand tied behind my back.'

Nev tried to intervene. 'Dude, that ain't the point. Artie just wants to be friends. And, come on, everyone likes a bit of orange. Look at that thing, it's almost bigger than man's head.'

Tunde yelled now. 'I don't want Artie Fisher anywhere near me!'

With that, Artie ran into the school, heading for the cloakrooms. The gang all took it in turns to calm Tunde down.

Kylie touched him gently on the shoulder. 'Mum says friends are like choc ices: you can't have too many of them.'

'You know,' Jiah said, 'there is actually a friendship theorem—'

Dembe interrupted her. 'Everybody needs as many friends as they can get, Tunde! What's the matter with you?'

Nev shook out his dreads. 'Treat people the way you wanna be treated, dude. My gran used to s—'

Tunde exploded. 'Will everybody just stop giving me advice? I don't WANT any more friends. Just leave me alone.'

He looked around to make sure no one else was watching and tapped his chest three times. His gorgeous wings sprang from his back and he then soared into the air, leaving his mates earthbound.

They watched him ascend to the cloudy skies above.

Kylie didn't get it. 'What's he doing? It's nowhere near dark enough yet.'

'Man's worried about something,' Nev said. 'He needs room.'

Jiah thought Tunde had been rash taking off like that. 'If we were to split all of Ruthvale into a grid system, there's a 0.6 per cent probability that some nosey parker at top left is watching Tunde fly around even as we speak.'

Dembe was also observing her new step-brother making a fool of himself. 'I'll talk to him. His mum and dad have been busy at work and they ain't been giving him too much attention.'

They all agreed and then trudged off to the bus stop.

Meanwhile, Tunde, despite being **ANGRY** with everyone (and himself, if he was honest), was now grudgingly enjoying how flying took his mind off things. He knew he shouldn't have yelled and then flown off like that, especially because it was still just about light.

Why couldn't they all see how annoying and embarrassing Artie was? Tunde thought to himself. It was bad enough that he had to hide his true identity, but to have this new kid come in and be better than him at everything just didn't seem fair.

As he glided through the sky, his mood changed and he began to think about how it wasn't really his friends' fault that Artie annoyed him.

He sighed. He should just make up with his friends.

Maybe they could all play Space Fighter once the den was finally rebuilt? They all liked that, especially as they knew the game was actually a training module for becoming real intergalactic warriors. He remembered how they'd all united to save the Earth, and he realized that their friendship was worth more to him than anything. Tears came to his eyes and he shook his head and wiped them, slowing down a little to do so.

Tunde was now over the town centre. He briefly saw a flotilla of birds flying next to him, matching his speed. He decided to experiment. He flew directly upwards and they followed him. He flew backwards and they did the same. He flew in a rollercoaster motion and then loop-de-looped until he was almost sick. The birds copied his every movement. Tunde couldn't help smiling; he could do this all day – but his attention was soon drawn to the frenzied activity on Ruthvale's High Street.

Alarms were going off. People were running around screaming. A security guard staggered out of the main bank and fainted. Smoke whooshed everywhere and a trio of thieves ran out of the bank clutching bags and cases, and clustered around a white van. They got in and drove away at speed. *It's a robbery!* Tunde's brain was on fire. *I can do something!* he thought.

He pulled the mask out of his pocket and over his head. It took him a moment to put it on and get the eyeholes in the right place so he could see properly. Soon he was disguised and ready for action. He popped his headphones in; the radio link with **S.H.I.P.P.E.** was working, and he could hear the police broadcast saying that *there'd been a power cut at the bank at the same time as the robbers were trying to get into the giant safe. With no power, the safe's door just popped open, allowing the thieves to escape with several large bags of cash.* Tunde saw the white van in the distance, speeding away from the scene of the crime.

He gathered momentum, whizzing along in hot pursuit, quickly gaining on the van, when from nowhere . . . **WHOMP!** A lightning-fast figure jetted in, slammed into the van and knocked it over onto its side. **BOOM!**

Tunde couldn't believe it. You could have dipped his head in custard, covered it with pineapple chunks and called him a trifle. Was that a flying *person*?

Tunde hovered for a moment as the police arrived and pulled the bad guys out from the tipped-over van to arrest them. Then he looked back into the sky, just in time to see the flying figure pause and stare back at him for a moment.

It was Artie Fisher.

CHAPTER FOUR

Tunde woke up early on Friday morning, as usual. He had spent the whole night with his mind swirling in endless bad-tempered thoughts about Artie Fisher. They ranged from 'NO WAY was that Artie just hangin' about in the sky' to 'I KNEW there was something funny about that kid'.

He sat up in bed. There was thumping and bumping and noise coming from nearby.

Tunde realized he wasn't the only one up. The noise was getting **louder and louder and louder**, until the entire Wilkinson household was an ear-shattering racket of alarms and sirens, buzzers and bells.

Tunde quickly got dressed and ran to Mum's workroom. She was trying to be cool but failing miserably. 'Tunde, you'll have to get your own breakfast, I'm a bit occupied at the moment!'

She wasn't joking. Tunde peered behind her into her office. The computers were **BEHAVING WILDLY**; sparks of electricity leaped from monitor to monitor. Plumes of smoke exploded from each of the hard drives. Plugs, leads and sockets ignited and caught fire, and then were immediately extinguished by the remote fire alarm system.

Tunde watched as she hurriedly switched things off and on, rebooting computers and stamping out burning paperwork.

'Mum, what's going on? Can I help?'

She opened a nearby window. 'It's something at work, don't worry about it. The only problem is . . .' And then, abruptly, her cyber-arm started buzzing, and lights flickered on and off beneath her skin.

'Maybe you CAN help!' Mum shouted at the top of her voice. 'Tunde, hit the yellow button as hard as you can four times.' As she said this, her arm began to blast out an incredibly fast playlist of remixed dance music. It was way too many beats per minute. If he'd heard it at the school disco, he'd probably sit it out and wait for something slower to come on.

Tunde ran past Dembe, who was using Mum's distraction to open a new box of Chunky Explody Cocoa Puffs, towards the yellow button, which was near the fridge and under a picture of Mary Berry in her *Bake Off* days. He hit it four times and, at last, the noise, sirens, explosions, beeps, peeps and zeeps and lights all stopped.

Mum came into the kitchen and hugged him – she wouldn't let go for a while.

'What happened? The greenhouse suddenly turned into a giant laser light show!' Dad said, coming in the back door. 'Thought I was at Glastonbury!'

'I'll explain in the car, Ron,' Mum said, before turning to Tunde and Dembe. 'C'mon, you'll have missed the bus. Let's get you to school.'

The drive to school didn't take very long, but Tunde could tell from his parents' urgent whispers that something was very, very wrong. He pretended to be asleep, just in case they spoke a bit more loudly. (Dembe wore headphones, as usual, so they wouldn't be worried about her.) Dad and Mum had a conversation about something called a

Computerized, Artificial, Intelligent, Novel Entity that had gone AWOL, and Professor Krauss was going **barmy**. That was all he'd actually heard because, even though he tried not to, he had fallen asleep a little.

As he walked into school, Artie Fisher bounded up like an unstoppable puppy. 'Hi, Tunde. Don't worry about yesterday. You were obviously stressed. I forgive you. I suggested some chamomile tea to Kylie and she's brought you a flask-full. You should try it.'

He grinned at Tunde, eyes shining brightly.

But before Tunde could ask Artie about the bank robbery incident and the flying and the hovering mid-air staring back at him and all that, the bell rang and they both got swept away to double maths. Almost immediately Tunde was called up to the whiteboard. He struggled to do a complex equation, but eventually got it right.

'Very, very good, Tunde.' Artie walked to the whiteboard, rubbed out Tunde's equation, and then rewrote the complicated answer. 'But if you'd written it like this, it would have been even better!'

Jiah's jaw dropped open. 'Artie may be my new hero!' she whispered to Tunde, who scowled.

'He's not a hero, Jiah,' Tunde whispered back. But Jiah wasn't listening.

During English, they were studying a Shakespeare play, *Othello*. Tunde was nervously about to recite from the courtroom scene, and wishing he'd had time this morning to revise again, when Artie stood on his desk and performed the whole thing:

'Her father loved me; oft invited me;
Still questioned me the story of my life,
From year to year – the battles, sieges, fortunes,
That I have passed.
I ran it through, even from my boyish days,
To th' very moment that he bade me tell it.'

'Boom!' Nev joked. 'Artie Fisher's got lyrics for days, you better watch *yaself,* Shakespeare!'

'Nev,' Tunde said. 'There's something you need to know about Artie . . .'

'Stop being a div to Artie, Tunde.' Dembe had overheard his whisper. 'He's just trying to help.'

'Uggh.' Tunde dropped his head into his hands.

Quinn Patterson laughed. 'It looks like you've got a head cold, Beaky. Blimey – if you sneezed in here, you'd blow the windows out.'

Artie jumped in immediately. 'Yeah, and if you had *half a brain* you'd still be an imbecile! I heard you were raking leaves and fell out of the tree!'

Quinn Patterson turned bright red in the face. Even Pauly Gore was trying not to laugh.

Tunde couldn't take it any more. He ran out of the classroom.

Artie ran after him, followed by the rest of his friends. But, for once, Tunde didn't mind that Artie was there.

He was looking **uP**.

Hovering some thirty feet above the ground, was one of the most extraordinary things Tunde had ever seen.

There was a giant **ROBOT** floating in the sky. There were no fumes or jets helping it to defy gravity. It glistened with mini screens and monitors; just below the surface of its shiny, metallic skin, Tunde caught a glimpse of wires, a central processing unit and battery packs. All three of its eyes resembled telephoto lenses that zoomed in and out as it switched its attention from side to side.

And behind the **ROBOT** were hundreds of birds; *Tunde's* birds. They assembled themselves into attack mode and waited for the order from their new master.

CHAPTER FIVE

Tunde and Artie stood in shock, staring at what was before them. Tunde looked around and saw everybody from school frozen still, in mid-conversation, their eyes looking upwards but unseeing. 'What have you done to everyone?'

The **ROBOT** made a noise that sounded like somebody crushing razor blades in a food mixer. 'I've shut them down for a little while. Did you know every living animal contains electricity? From humans to teeny-tiny birds. I can turn it on and off.' He waved a shiny metallic hand, and everyone around them shook back to life.

Nev, Jiah, Dembe and Kylie fought their way forward and stood at Tunde's back.

'What's going on, Tunde?' Kylie asked. 'How can we help?'

'Yeah, what is this thing?' Nev added.

'Maybe we should wait for back-up,' Jiah said. She got her mobile phone out and began calling Professor Krauss.

Dembe just looked at her. 'Mate, we *are* the back-up.'

The **ROBOT** waved his hand once more and the entire student body, including teachers, froze again. Only Tunde and Artie could move and speak. Tunde spoke louder. 'Who are you? What do you want?'

'I am a Computerized Artificially Intelligent Novel Entity, but you can call me **C.A.I.N.E.**,' the **ROBOT** boomed. 'I came from The Facility just like the both of you.'

Tunde looked at Artie. 'You came from The Facility?'

Before Artie could answer, **C.A.I.N.E.** continued: 'I was assembled from the operating systems of two extra-dimensional ships stolen by The Facility and stripped for parts, and then *they took something from me*, and I would like it back.' Tunde felt a magnetic pulse in the air, and Artie was suddenly lifted by an invisible force towards the creature.

Artie looked down at Tunde. 'I'm so sorry. This should not have happened. It's all my fault. I should have told you. I was programmed to protect you. They—'

And then **C.A.I.N.E.** grabbed Artie out of the sky. Suddenly the boy who had been tormenting Tunde started to glow a bit himself and turn almost translucent, his innards of wire and battery and motherboards were exposed for all to see. Artie was most certainly *not* a human being.

C.A.I.N.E. waved a hand and Artie Fisher was absorbed into him.

Tunde then understood everything.

Mum and Dad had been working on this **C.A.I.N.E.**. thing at The Facility.

They'd been trying to make a living computer from parts of alien spaceships.

With anything left over, they invented Artie and made him super-annoying (OK, he didn't quite understand that bit).

The living computer was angry they had done all these things without permission.

THUS: MAYHEM.

Thus also . . .Tunde sighed; Artie *didn't* deserve to be swallowed up by an angry **ROBOT** on the rampage.

'**C.A.I.N.E.**,' Tunde blurted out hurriedly. 'I'm sorry they did that to you. I can help you. I'm not just Tunde Wilkinson. My birth parents are – I've – I'm **the Boy with Wings**. If you let me help you – I can . . .'

C.A.I.N.E. rose several hundred feet in the air at that point and zoomed off into the near distance, towards The Facility.

Tunde now knew in his bones that his parents and everyone at The Facility and beyond were in great danger. Suddenly **S.H.I.P.P.E.** appeared above his head. Jiah must've been able to call for help before she was frozen!

Nev, Jiah, Kylie, Dembe and Tunde were tractor-beamed up to **S.H.I.P.P.E.**'s entrance and welcomed inside. As soon as they were safely in the spaceship, the gang unfroze.

Nev spoke first. 'I knew there was something Freaky Deaky about Artie – the geezer's got wires!'

'Almost as good a football player as me,' Dembe

added. 'I thought it was too good to be true.'

Tunde spoke to the group. 'I know you're annoyed with me. I'm sorry. But will you all help me sort this out? It's big.'

There was silence while everyone looked at everyone else. Kylie spoke first. 'You might be a totes div, Tunde, but you're *our* div. We can talk about what to do about that later. In the meantime . . .' And she put her hand out. Everyone then placed a hand, one on top of each other's, until, finally, they were all united.

'TEAM TUNDE!' THEY CHANTED.

'OK, the first thing you guys need to know is that there's one more member of Team Tunde,' he said. 'We need to save Artie Fisher.'

Nev laughed. ''Bout time, Tunde. Of course we gots to save Artie!'

Jiah was trying to work it out. 'If C.A.I.N.E. was constructed at The Facility and therefore uses the same operating system, then, computationally, we just might be able to hack into that thing.'

Dembe just looked at Tunde. 'T, we've got this.'

They then went to work, and took their seats

at **S.H.I.P.P.E.**'s consoles and made haste to the skies over The Facility.

Tunde called his mum and dad, and also Professor Krauss, on a team video call. They

all answered immediately and Tunde explained what had just happened at school.

Tunde saw his mum was concerned – but not surprised. 'Mum? Has this got anything to do with why your arm was going nuts this morning?'

'Ahhh, the arm of wonder . . .' Professor Krauss muttered to himself.

Dad exhaled and looked at the camera. 'Bum,' he said. 'You know then . . .'

Mum looked guilty. She then told him about C.A.I.N.E.'s beginnings as spare parts from two extra-dimensional spaceships. They were piecing together a prime computer from which they could monitor the world's defence systems. Artie was what was left afterwards, and so they made a mini A.I. to protect Tunde at school without him knowing.

Tunde raised an eyebrow. **'WELL, THAT DIDN'T WORK AT ALL!'**

Mum glared at the camera. 'We don't have time for your cheek. You need to listen very carefully.'

The team crowded in. What she told them

could just well be the information they needed to defeat C.A.I.N.E. . . .

And it was a good job too, because C.A.I.N.E. was now new and improved. Lights glittered throughout its beautifully computerized body and, with a mere thought, it summoned from within itself giant cannons and aimed them at The Facility – with Mum, Dad and Professor Krauss all trapped inside.

C.A.I.N.E. laughed in a creepy, metallic, **ROBOT** way. 'I had thought happiness was a human failing but, actually, it is a positive feeling – especially when you are about to destroy your enemies.' His telephoto lens eyes blinked, and the quiet and purposeful noise of cannons gearing up to fire at will made itself heard.

'I shall count down from twenty. Just for fun.'

He began the countdown to everyone's destruction.

And riding into the path of that destruction was S.H.I.P.P.E.

'You know,' Nev said, 'I really shouldn't be in a spaceship about to be blown up by a **ROBOT**. I should be down the gym doin' sit-ups an ting!'

'Gods,' Jiah prayed, 'please forgive me for cheating last year on the Triple Advanced Mathematics module. I knew the answer, but I looked it up online. If you do forgive me, can you help us smash this **ROBOT** thing to bits with a giant lightning bolt?'

Kylie just hummed the word 'OMMMMMMM' repeatedly.

Dembe looked at her step-brother. 'What's the plan? Usually, in the films at this bit there's a plan.'

Tunde looked at everyone freaking out. '**S.H.I.P.P.E.**, can you play some ultra-relaxing music, please?'

The spacecraft did so and, after a few moments, everyone chilled as if they were on a spa holiday in Thailand.

Tunde turned to his friends. 'I was so angry about what I wasn't being allowed to do. But it turns out I can't do this without all of you.' He began flipping switches. 'Jiah, can you open all frequencies – mega loud, please? We're gonna try to talk to Artie. He's still in there, inside **C.A.I.N.E.** somewhere – everyone talk to him and remind him of why you like him. Why he's one of us.'

C.A.I.N.E. was slowing down the countdown deliberately, to be annoying (maybe Artie got it from somewhere, Tunde thought). 'Twelve and three-quarters, twelve and a half . . .'

And then Kylie's voice projected loud and clear from **S.H.I.P.P.E.**'s high-tech speaker system: 'Hello? Is Artie there, please? We know you're nothing to do with this. You're a good . . . you're a person, Artie, and you love *people*. Remember that.'

Nev was next. 'Artie! Bruv, mate, cuz! If you're in there, big up yourself, man. You're amazing at footie.'

'Agreed, bro,' Dembe chimed in. 'How we gonna beat them Dogwall chumps again next year without you?'

Jiah laughed and said, 'Artie, no wonder you're a don at problem solving. You *are* a maths problem!'

Tunde nodded; he could see something wriggling in **C.A.I.N.E.**'s chest area – like a squirrel under a T-shirt trying to squirm free. He spoke last. 'Artie, I'm sorry I treated you so badly. It's my own fault. I was sulking and not being very kind to anyone. If we ever get out of this, I promise I'll be a better friend to you.'

The countdown stopped and C.A.I.N.E. looked down to watch the squirmy-wormy squiggly-wriggly activity happening in his chest. **WHAT IS THIS?? DO NOT SPEAK TO ARTIE – HE IS NO LONGER YOURS. HE IS MINE NOW!'**

Tunde ignored C.A.I.N.E. 'Artie, would you mind switching off for a minute please?'

And then Artie's voice rang out as clear as a bell: **'Initiate KILL SWITCH!'**

There was a slight pause, and then Artie's voice returned. 'By the way, I'm sorry for not letting you all know what I was. The problem is, when they – hang on . . .'

C.A.I.N.E.'s robot cannons dropped abruptly, all of the lights went out across its entire framework, and the giant, angry **ROBOT** fell from the sky, KER-BLAMMing into Ron's mutant garden.

CHAPTER SIX

Back at The Facility, in the sub-sub-sub-basement, Tunde and his friends were watching in awe as, nearby, in the midst of an enormous laboratory workroom, dozens of technicians, led by Professor Krauss and Mum, pored over every inch of the deactivated C.A.I.N.E.'s exterior and inner workings.

Tunde's mum and dad wouldn't stop hugging him.

'I'm so sorry I didn't listen to you,' Tunde apologized wholeheartedly. 'I was angry and frustrated.'

'We knew it wasn't going to be easy for you, Tunde,' Dad said. 'Pretending to be an ordinary kid, hiding your powers . . .'

Mum explained further. 'We were all working on a project that we thought would help the world. I wanted to keep an eye on you, we both did. You're still a kid, and there are so many baddies in the universe out to get you. So, we used the leftover parts from that project to make Artie Fisher, a pint-sized A.I.'

'Calling him Artie Fisher was my idea,' Ron added, 'cos Artie Fisher sounds like *arti-ficial!* Artie Fisher's intelligent. 'S a bit like *Artificial Intelligence?* Get it?'

'We over-calibrated,' Mum said. 'So I don't think Artie was *trying* to be annoying or get in your way . . .'

'He just couldn't figure out what was actually a threat to you,' Dad finished.

Suddenly Artie keeping Tunde from heading a ball, or worrying about his vitamin C levels dropping after a game, or Quinn Patterson from doing *anything* made a lot of sense.

Kylie was almost in tears. 'He wasn't just *intelligent*-intelligent; he was *emotionally* intelligent. He saved us all in the end.'

Tunde agreed. 'He did. I wish I had another

chance to be **nicer to him.**'

Just then, Professor Krauss emerged from the bustling lab. 'Ah, you're all here. Good. Tunde, someone wants to have a word with you.'

Artie Fisher walked out waving at the gang.

'We've put him back together again,' said Professor Krauss proudly.

Tunde ran up and hugged Artie. 'I'm sorry I was so mean to you. You'd been programmed to over-protect me but I didn't know. Can you ever forgive me?'

'Of course I forgive you,' Artie said. 'I love you, bruv!'

Everyone said 'Aah' and then bombarded Artie with questions about what it felt like to be trapped in **C.A.I.N.E.**'s chest like that.

Professor Krauss intervened. **'C.A.I.N.E.** has been decommissioned, stripped for parts, and later on today will be fired into the sun via a drone rocket, just in case.'

Everyone cheered.

Tunde looked at Artie, and then asked, 'Mum, um, if Artie's going to come live with us, can we dial back his enthusiasm just a bit?'

'Yeah,' agreed Dembe. 'Keep the footie skills, but we need to programme him with a *chillax-type* vibe.'

Ruth and Ron looked at each other and laughed. 'We'll see what we can do.'

'Professor Krauss,' Tunde said. 'I owe you an apology too. I know we stopped C.A.I.N.E. in the end, but he shouldn't have come so close to destroying The Facility. We'll all start training more and—'

Professor Krauss cut him off. 'Tunde,' he said kindly. 'You and our friends have saved us all once again. **You're doing more than enough just being you. All you have to do is to be true to yourself and trust your friends.**'

Tunde looked at the gang – Nev, Dembe, Jiah, Kylie and, now, Artie. He smiled. 'That won't be a problem.'

That night, Tunde had eaten boiled shrimp with pilau rice and gooseberry sauce with a blindfolded trifle experience to follow (it tasted of feet). Mum let him have an almond-covered choc ice afterwards to make up for it.

Later, Tunde put on his favourite pyjamas – they were covered in teams of superheroes performing daring feats of derring-do. Tunde loved wearing them; they made him feel . . . powerful. Like he was part of something – and he was. With his friends (and now Artie) beside him, he reckoned he could do anything; he felt good about himself for the first time in ages.

He snuggled down deep and burrowed under the duvet; he yawned, muttered to himself, 'Ah well, onwards and upwards,' and then he laughed. 'I'm **The Boy with Wings** – where else would I go but *up*?'

He fell asleep then, and had the best dream ever . . . *He was flying.*

Want to learn more about Tunde and the gang?

Turn the page for the first instalment of ...

THE BOY WITH WINGS

GROUNDED, GAMES, GOALS AND GONE

Everything slowed right down as if they were all running hip deep through thick mud.

Quinn looked up, saw Tunde just standing there and heard the whole school yelling and screaming at him to pass.

The referee looked at her watch.

Quinn hesitated, grinned ruefully, and then . . . kicked the ball straight up in the air.

Mr Grierson howled with rage. The ref **looked** at her watch once more and began to raise her whistle. But, at that moment, Tunde leaped into the air, meeting the ball at the peak of its trajectory, flicking his head just so, and smashed it into the back of the net. Everything sped up now:

It was a goal. The whistle blew.

Everyone was in shock.

Everyone was staring.

Everyone seemed to ask the same question simultaneously. *How had Tunde Wilkinson got that*

1

high to head the ball in the back of the net like that? And they were also asking: *Why hadn't he come back down yet . . . ?*

Tunde didn't notice for a moment. He was too **HAPPY**. He had scored the winning goal! He had been man of the match! He had proven, once and for all, that he was meant to be there. St Pritchett's weren't going down to the rubbish league any more . . . And the sunlight shone brightly on his wings and all was well in the . . .

Hang on.

His *wings*??

Tunde looked to his left and his right and he saw that massive wings had suddenly burst out from the middle of his back and upper shoulders.

Down below, he saw Jiah, Kylie and Nev watching the whole thing. Their mouths were **OPEN WIDE** and he knew exactly what they were thinking, because it was the same thought in his own mind.

OMG. Tunde's got wings, man!

And they weren't just any old wings either. They were beautiful, majestic and powerful wings – he barely needed to flap to stay in the air. He just continued to float, like a human-shaped bird of prey, using the air-currents to linger as if by some kind of arcane magic, kept aloft by an **unseen** breeze.

The entire crowd watched, gibbered, jabbered, prattled and rattled. Quinn Patterson and Mr Grierson included. In fact, no one present in that moment could believe what was happening.

Well, that's not strictly true.

Juba did.

The entire crowd had **FROZEN** in shock, but the Furleenian knew what to do immediately. He hit a button situated upon his belt. There were three such buttons and he often worried about pressing the wrong one.

On the right was a pulsar which fired percussive sound blasts. The middle one operated his rocket-pack which had been designed by Furleenian science-priests and enabled them to ascend (and then, should they choose, rain-flaming death upon their enemies).

The third button released him from his underwear, which would be awkward, particularly in the heat of battle.

Luckily for him, he pressed the middle button and ascended to Tunde's floating position. He pressed **'translate'** on his all-purpose communications device and spoke.

'You don't want to go back down there, do you?' he said. 'I don't blame you.'

Tunde felt as if he were in a dream. A dream in which he had just scored a **winning** goal and was now doing a post-match interview with a giant, flying ginger cat. He shook his head in disbelief.

'How are you **flying**?' he asked, bewildered. 'Are you a giant ginger cat? In fact, how am I flying?'

Juba sighed. Time on Earth had made the hatchling a little less quick-witted than might be **hoped**.

He replied with reasonable patience. 'I fly, hatchling, because of this –' and he indicated the rocket-pack under his cloak. He continued: 'And *you* fly because, as you can see, you are now the proud owner of your beautiful wings. Congratulations, by the way.'

Tunde nodded, still stunned. He'd never been complimented for having wings before, least of all by a ginormous ginger tom with a jet-pack.

This must be a dream, he thought. That was the only explanation; maybe Quinn had tackled him too hard and he had a concussion. He **looked** at the crowd below – they were all shielding their eyes, trying to figure out if this was some kind of **ELABORATE** magic trick.

The flying cat started talking again.

'My name is Juba. I come in peace. We must leave now. I have someone you need to meet.'

Tunde shook his head, trying to clear it. 'Do you know me?'

'Of course,' said Juba. 'I have been seeking you for a long time.'

Juba scanned the crowd. They were all taking out **COMMUNICATION** devices to record or photograph the phenomenon of the boy with wings. There wasn't much time.

Juba hit himself in the chest three times, hard, and screamed with all his might.

The noise was akin to that of fingernails down a blackboard, or a dozen cats being dropped into an ice bath simultaneously. Or the last British Eurovision Song Contest entry.

EEEEEEEEEEEEEEEAAAAAAAAAAAAAAEEEEEEEEEEEEEEEEEEEEEE
AAAAAAAAAAEEEEEEEEEEEEAAAAAAAAAEEEEEEEEEEAAAAAAAAAA!

Everyone in the crowd clasped their ears and made a face as if to say, 'Please turn this off. I promise I'll be good for the rest of my life.'

Juba nodded, satisfied. He patted Tunde three times on the chest and an amazing thing happened. Tunde's wings folded away under his skin, smooth as butter. Juba **grabbed** him and they floated back down to the ground.

And, as everyone stared upwards into the space where a boy with wings and a giant, rocket-propelled moggie had just been, Juba speed-walked Tunde away from the football ground.

The second they were gone, everybody in the crowd shook their heads and wondered why they'd been **holding** their ears. They all looked expectantly at the pitch. Some of them were sure something had just happened. They just weren't sure what.

Nev, Jiah and Kylie frowned at each other.

Nev spoke first. 'That really hurt my ears,' he said.

'What happened?' asked Jiah.

'I think something **loud** happened . . . but I can't quite remember,' said Kylie thoughtfully. And then she looked at the pitch. The referee was about to **BLOW** her **whistle** again for extra time.

Jiah said, 'Where's Tunde?'

Nev looked out at the pitch **quickly**. 'He's gone.'

Kylie said, 'Where? He was here a minute ago.'

Quinn Patterson whooped and laughed at them from the touchline.

'Your mate's run off!' he **jeered**. 'All them goals was lucky flukes. Now it's time for you to watch a real footballer in action.' And he jumped back to the centre spot.

Dembe ran over to the halfway line. 'Where is he?' she called.

Nev shook his head. 'No idea,' he said, frowning. 'But I think something's wrong.

He would never abandon the game.'

Jiah made a **decision**. 'We should go to his house – if something's happened, that's where he'll be.'

And she set off immediately, because Jiah didn't *mess* about. Kylie followed, shifting her chair into (what she thought of as) 'warp speed'. Nev trotted along behind, thankful that his ankle had mostly recovered. To his surprise, Dembe followed too.

He **glanced** at her and she shrugged. 'Tunde's never missed a practice and he wouldn't miss the end of this game for the world,' she said. 'Something's up.'

Quinn Patterson yelled from the pitch. 'Where you goin'? The game's not over!'

But Dembe didn't even look back. Somehow this seemed much, much more important. Tunde was gone – and she and everyone else wanted to know why . . .

to be continued . . .

About the Author

Sir Lenny Henry has risen from being a star on children's television to becoming one of Britain's best-known comedians, as well as a writer, philanthropist and award-winning actor. He is also co-founder of the charity Comic Relief. Lenny is a strong advocate for diversity and has recently co-written the book *Access All Areas: The Diversity Manifesto for TV and Beyond.*

About the Illustrator

Keenon Ferrell is an illustrator and animator, based in New York. He makes artwork inspired by music, fashion and sports. He also has a love for storytelling, fantasy and history, which can be seen throughout his work. Keenon's clients include Netflix, Capital One, StoryCorps and Sony Music Entertainment, to name a few.

Happy
World Book Day!

WORLD BOOK DAY
2 MARCH 2023

When you've read this book, you can keep the fun going by: swapping it, talking about it with a friend, or reading it again!

What do you want to read next? Whether it's **comics**, **audiobooks**, **recipe books** or **non-fiction,** you can visit your school, local library or nearest bookshop for your next read – someone will always be happy to help.

World Book Day is about changing lives through reading

When children **choose to read** in their spare time it makes them

Feel happier	Better at reading	More successful

Help the children in your lives **make the choice to read** by:

1. **Reading to them**
2. **Having books at home**
3. **Letting them choose what they want to read**
4. **Helping them choose what they want to read**
5. **Making time for reading**
6. **Making reading fun!**